Stories from the Underworld
By Johanna K. Pitcairn

Copyright 2013, 2014 Johanna K. Pitcairn
All rights reserved

License Notes

TABLE OF CONTENTS

Foreword

The world is a strange place. If you look around closely, you might find things that will scare the shit out of you. But who are we truly without fear? Embark on a journey and never look back. You might just land in a peaceful haven, who knows?

My dear thanks to Minnie for sticking around no matter how scary the world looks to her (and me). Thanks to Mom and Dad for loving me unconditionally. Thanks to God for always watching over me. Thanks to past and future friends, known and unknown, for their advice and help. I'm indefinitely grateful.

To thine own self be true. Never forget that.

J.K.P.

Open Letter To A Kindred Spirit

Dear Friend,

You probably have no idea who I am. You're maybe wondering whether I've lost my mind, and am looking to "get my ass kicked" by you, or one of your fellows, because it will teach me a good lesson. I hope it's not too presumptuous in wanting to be friends. Yes, I would like for us to establish a friendly relationship. Why? Well, I'll tell you why.

For many years I've lived under a fake identity. I've pretended to be like everyone else, really, I was totally boring. I went to work, bought groceries, acted polite and respectful with strangers, even took out the trash every evening… because that was what I was supposed to do, right?

You know… I've learned many things during the few years I discovered my true nature, and it changed the whole picture. I saw the world with new eyes, and it excited me; it actually drove me insane to be honest. I rejected my feelings at the beginning… of course, that was totally normal, given the circumstances. I mean, how did you feel the first time you realized you liked to do that to people? *Exactly.* Well at least, you didn't feel guilty, which is a plus in my playbook. No guilt allows letting go of all the stress, without worrying about the consequences.

I am weird. I enjoy what I do. There's nothing better than this. *Such a beautiful gift.* I live far away from people. Kidding. New York City is an exquisite playground, but you knew this already. It's really easy to deceive people into believing I'm such a nice and helpful neighbor. I like to have my little secrets. They're mine… *forever*. I don't even need a photo album. I can remember each of them so vividly. Ah… Let me contemplate this for a second… Yes. That's right. Perfect.

I know how you feel, deep inside. I know about the anger. It's very slight at first, but then it grows, like a big tornado, and sweeps everything away so quickly. I like my anger. You want to know how I started? This I must tell you because it really is fascinating.

I was dating this girl, you see, and she was a bit annoying. Always nagging me, asking me to do things with such an irritating tone of voice, oh... But I didn't let her get to me that easily, no... I waited. It didn't take very long for her to become a real bitch, she wasn't that shrewd to begin with. So I bought this very nice hair dryer as a birthday present for her... and she threw it in my face, said I had no interest in her anymore... She wanted to leave me. That felt funny when she said that. Anyway, I let her talk, and once she was done, I looked at her, and smiled. She slapped me, asking me why I was grinning like an "insensitive moron". I responded that she needed to take a bath... She was dirty. She thought I was acting weird but complied after I smiled some more. And off to the bathtub she went. I massaged her shoulders and washed her hair. I took my time, you know.

I never like to rush things. She smelt so sweet, a pure delight. She even forgot about the whole argument. When I asked her to dress herself, she went to the bedroom, and I started cleaning the bathroom. *I am very meticulous.* Then I told her I would dry her hair, and she looked very surprised, but she complied. Again. Women are so... easy to manipulate. I never lost my temper, no, I stayed very calm. She didn't seem nervous at all. It all went according to plan. I made her sit on a stool, and proceeded to switch on the hair dryer. It made a lot of noise; it was hard to hear her speak. But she had nothing interesting to say, so I nodded without listening. She was smiling. I kept staring at her reflection in the bathroom mirror. She acted like a little girl, so vulnerable...

I really take my time. I wanted her to look perfect. Her hair was gorgeous, by the way... I watched her sitting there. So lovely. Really, she was. That's when I knew the moment was right. When I finished my masterpiece, she had nothing to say anymore. It felt so good, not to hear her fucking voice! I was so proud of my work. There was nothing to see but a beautiful baby doll... So beautiful.

I tied a scarf around her neck to hide the hideous cord mark, and then moved her to a more comfortable chair in the living room. Who said the dead can't be comfortable? She looked stunning. All dressed up, with her hair done, and this smile, this smile that never left her face. What a memory.

Anyway, that anger... I think it's my best friend, you know... *So... I'm like you.* We should exchange personal information if you come across that letter, and I'd love to hear your impressions. You must have so many novel ideas.

So wonderful, isn't it? This sense of peace after a good hunt… There's really nothing like it.

Well, I'll be on my way now. Let's chat later, if you're interested, of course. We could always grab a drink sometime.

Cheers my future friend. And beware.

It's quite a jungle out there.

Sincerely,

The boy next door.

The Horse

A bad dream. It was all a bad dream. Laura poked the belly of the animal to make sure it was dead. How could she continue her journey to the Dome without a ride? No way she'd hitchhike with all the whackos and criminals wandering the streets since the sun stopped shining five days earlier, right when she celebrated her eighteenth birthday. Talk about a lucky day.

Her best friend Julie had organized the perfect party for her in the basement of her parents' house while they were on vacation. Five guys, five girls, alcohol, LSD and ecstasy, good music and twelve hours to kill… A real blast. Laura woke up feeling the weight of an arm on her chest, and when she opened her eyes, realized the arm belonged to John. He was sweet, cute, mostly sweet, no, mostly cute… She loved to stare into his bright blue eyes and lose herself thinking she could be his girlfriend until the end of the year. Maybe they could go to prom together and have sex. It was a big deal and she wanted John to be her first one. She wouldn't regret it if he gave her her first sexual experience, because she knew it deep down he would be fantastic in bed.

Far memories, long gone down a drain of nonsense. Laura bowed her head and tried to contain her anger while walking away from the horse that had collapsed under her. That freaking horse was a piece of crap, just like everything else she found on her way to the Dome. Her friends, yeah "friends", had ditched her after stealing a car and John, this jerk, had also split without taking her with him. He said he had to reach the Dome before it was too late. How about their time together, didn't it mean anything at all? They had kissed and shared pills; she had let him slide his hand under her blouse. Such a waste. All she could manage to steal was this deadbeat horse - or was it a mere pony, she had no clue anymore - she spotted while passing down a field about three days ago. The animal offered no luxury but she needed to move faster, and the Dome was miles away. Did it really matter now how far the Dome was? Not really.

She had climbed up the stairs back to Julie's living room, still high from the night before, and noticed the sky had not changed color, yet it was ten in the morning. She didn't understand why the sun wasn't up, and blamed the LSD for altering her vision but what she considered a hallucination soon became an ugly truth to acknowledge. TV news reports kept repeating the same stuff: an experimental probe sent years ago by NASA to study the sun had exploded and caused the burning star to lose all its nuclear power. The last rays of light had reached the terrestrial surface while she was still asleep and dreaming of making sweet love to John, and now well, it would be night forever.

Shit. She angrily kicked a stone with her foot and cried in pain. She couldn't see anything, because in her hurry to reach the Dome, she had forgotten to take a flashlight. She felt cold, and her coat was too thin to keep her body temperature even. Tears rolled down her cheeks but she ignored them. Maybe she would have to hitchhike after all.

She twisted her head and looked behind her, hoping to see car lights in the distance but the road sadly remained clear of any living soul. All she could see was the dust of the desert dancing in little swirls over the asphalt. Staring at the dark sky, she blinked at stars bursting through the heavy cloak like diamonds. The deadly temperature forced her to sneeze, causing her snot to instantly freeze onto her nose.

She suddenly heard the sound of an engine roar in the distance. She saw a vehicle approaching and ran to the middle of the road, waving her arms at the driver to make him halt.

"You need help?" the old man behind the wheel asked while pulling down his window. Laura saw a shape in the passenger seat next to him.

"I'm going to the Dome," she said.

"We'd take ya but how d'we know ya ain't gonna kill us?" the voice of a woman replied.

"I don't have a weapon."

"How d'ya come up here?" the man asked.

"On a horse."

"Where's it now?" the woman followed.

"Dead."

The old man didn't respond and whispered something to his female companion.

"We got n'thing to eat, we take ya if ya show us the beast," he mumbled. "Ya walk, and I follow. Now go."

Laura headed to the ditch where the horse had collapsed an hour earlier. Her feet were aching and she hoped as hell this old couple wouldn't kill her after she led them to the animal. How did she know they could be trusted? She didn't. The car lights created a halo around her frame as the old man slowly drove behind her. She finally stopped walking when she recognized the body of the horse on the side of the road.

"Here," she said and the man turned off the engine.

"Get in," the old woman ordered, now pointing a twelve gauge sawed-off shotgun at Laura's head.

"Why you wanna shoot me?" Laura yelled, raising her hands above her head.

"Safety measure 'til we pull the horse inside the trunk. My Billy need t'cut it in pieces first, and meanwhile I gotta watch ya so you ain't got the right idea to become criminal on us. Now get in!"

Laura reluctantly moved toward the car, never losing sight of the gun pointed at her. She wouldn't survive very long if she rode with such hillbillies, but needed their car and their weapons if she wanted to reach the Dome alive and in one piece.

She slowly opened the back door and jumped in. The right moment for her escape would come soon enough... When Billy finished loading the last piece into the trunk, he sat behind the wheel and lit a cigarette.

"Good. Now we got one horse and one girl for dinner. Mary, take care of her for me, will ya?"

Laura felt a blow to her head before fully processing what the man just said, and everything turned black.

******

"*The criminal cop killing hip-hop filling minimal swap to cop millions of Pac listeners.*

Your coming with me, feel it or not you're gonna fear it like I showed you the spirit of god lives in us. You hear it a lot, lyrics the shock is it a miracle or am I just a product of pop fizzing up. For shizzle my whizzle this is the plot listen up you bizzles forgot slizzle does not give a fuck..."

The future was doomed and primitive needs had become paramount to everything else. Following the beam of his car lights, John shook his head to the beat and his foot pressed harder on the gas pedal. He needed to reach the Dome before running out of food and water, and the last gas station he passed had already been looted.

He didn't see another vehicle for miles, and almost came to the conclusion everybody who couldn't flee on time had died, until his attention shifted to a truck parked on the side of the road. The truck's bright warning blinkers were on. He hesitated about checking it out, and slammed on the brake pedal at the last possible second. His brains would have decorated the windshield in a nice festive way had he not been wearing his seatbelt.

He parked the stolen BMW a few feet ahead of the truck and grabbed the colt hidden in the glove compartment.

It was hard to see inside the truck given the huge amount of blood splattered on all the front windows. He carefully circled the vehicle and checked the rear to make sure nobody was ambushing him, before releasing the right back door handle. He pointed the gun at the opening, ready to shoot.

There was a body lying on the back seat. Two more sat in the front, their head reduced to mere pulp. John reached for the body's leg and received a kick.

"Can you breathe?" he asked, holding the colt with shaky hands.

"Help..." the body whispered.

John put the gun away and pulled the body by the legs. A girl. Her face was smeared with blood and half her hair stuck to her skin, but she seemed fine.

"Are you hurt?" John searched for a pulse.

The girl made inaudible sounds.

"I'll take you out of here, alright?" John ran his arm under her waist and carried her out of the truck back to the BMW.

After setting her up on the passenger seat, he checked the truck for supplies and found three sawed-off shotguns and a dead horse cut in a million pieces. No need to stick around any longer. He took the extra ammo and paced back to the BMW. Turning up the heat to the max, he glanced at the girl he rescued and wondered if it had been such a good idea to play Samaritan for once in his life. He stared closer at her face and felt like he knew her from somewhere, but she was covered in too much blood to tell exactly what she looked like.

Enough wasted time already. Time to roll off to the Dome.

"Soon as a verse starts I eat it at MC's heart, What is he thinking? How not to go against me? Smart. And it's absurd how people hang on every word. I'll probably never get the props I feel I ever deserve, But I'll never be served my spot is forever reserved, If I ever leave earth that would be the death of me first..."

******

They drove for hours. John had listened to the same CD over and over again and knew all the lyrics by heart.

He glanced from time to time at his passenger and tried to figure out who she reminded him of. The party at Julie's house felt like a mere blur, and he barely remembered making out with Laura and taking so many drugs he blacked out on the floor of the basement and woke up only to realize the sun had never risen. Once he entered the living room, he saw Laura running around like a frantic bug and tried to calm her down but she kept hitting him, unable to listen, lost in a confused state he chose not to witness while he could still run away without anyone noticing. After checking the news, he walked out and searched for a car he could borrow. He had never stolen something that big before, but if things worked out at the Dome he could maybe survive and give sense to the chaos that had so suddenly ruined his life. He didn't have a real plan about what he would like to do once there; he just needed to find a way out of this mess so he left. Laura cried and begged him to take her with him, but he couldn't handle a crazy girl on top of the end of the world as he knew it.

After several days, he realized he had been driving in the wrong direction. He had wasted precious time and had to turn back; how long would it be until he could find the right road to the Dome and not give up complete hope? Despite knowing the Dome existed, nobody told him exactly where it was located as the number of free spots was extremely limited. Like a lottery system, only the fittest could have access to a life away from darkness and certain death by starvation and hypothermia. He knew he could make it. If only he hadn't taken the wrong road, he would probably be there by now.

The girl seemed in shock. She had been sleeping for so long it he started to believe she would never wake up. How did the two other bodies die in the car? Did she shoot them? Was she their captive?

John sighed and tried to relax the muscles of his neck. He could feel the fatigue slowly taking him over, but he had to keep moving. No more time could be wasted.

******

John's head hurt like hell. He opened his eyes but couldn't see much ahead of him. Darkness everywhere. He also couldn't hear a thing besides his own breathing and his face felt wet.

Why was he not driving? The throbbing pulse of blood in his head made him dizzy. Was he upside down? His hand ran along the dashboard, searching for the glove box handle. He had to move slowly because his ribcage ached every time he exhaled and after a few seconds, took a break. He sat so close yet so far from the flashlight and the seatbelt prevented him from moving freely inside the vehicle. What if he unbuckled it?

Searching for the release button, he felt something warm. An arm. The girl next to him. Was she dead? He heard the dripping of blood on the ceiling and wondered the extent of his head injury. He couldn't panic now. Scalp wounds were supposed to bleed extensively. All he had to do was find the freaking seatbelt button and get out of the wreckage, and then could worry about the rest.

The Dome. How could he reach the Dome? Everything had turned to shit. Dammit. He landed right on his head when he finally got out of his harness. Ouch! The glove box. Once he held the flashlight he crawled out of the car.

Maybe not seeing anything was a better idea after all. A tree branch had pierced the windshield like butter and impaled his already wounded passenger right in the middle of the chest. Talk about a bloody spectacle. He didn't have time to think twice before emptying the content of his stomach on the side of the road. The retching lasted a while before he could look at the car again without feeling sick anymore. And now, what?

He quickly started to cough blood and the pain in his brain became unbearable, causing blurry vision and disturbing his balance. The coughing increased and he felt like air was missing. Maybe a broken rib had pierced one of his lungs?

Come on! The flashlight fell to the ground and John collapsed to his knees, catching a last breath of oxygen as he rolled to the side, his mouth stuck to the asphalt, his face covered in dirt and his eyes staring at the darkness, suddenly thinking of a severed horse head stuck in a trunk. Who cared about the end of the world? Where he was heading now, he needed no warmth and no hope.

The sun had stopped shining and the horse would be his last memory. Way to go, winner.

Animal

The world was spinning at the speed of light. The animal inside wanted out. His heart racing, he was ready to be untamed and unleashed, howling in the fading night, mating as if about to die. Pressing her hands firmly against his chest, he let out a last breath with a scream of pleasure. Her mouth gaped in response, leaving the void of her throat open to an army of flies dancing in hectic circles above her hollow face.

Her once beautiful smile was forever gone. Now she lay on a bed of straw, time slowly turning her to dust. Sitting by her side, he proceeded to trace lines on her parchment lips with his fingertips. He didn't care about her cadaverous appearance; he had promised her he'd love her forever. And loving her he did. He never stopped touching her, his memories acting like enticing pictures that truly spoke to his core.

She just kept fading more to his despair. The man could not let her go; she had been his for so long, what would he do without her? Tears fell onto her face as he kissed her. After days of starvation and sleepless nights, he finally succumbed to dreams that ravished his mind for hours; tossing and turning, his eyelids flickered with agitation. There, he could see her, and she was alive. She told him how much she loved him, and how much she missed him. Oh how stunning she looked! The most desirable woman he had ever met.

She spoke directly to his sexual being, and he implored her to stay. As he tried to grab her hand, she slowly glided away from his thoughts to be replaced with more salacious ideas. He wandered in a world filled with tubs of blood and severed body parts. His journey brought him to an empty operating room. There was a body on the steel table. There she remained, drop dead gorgeous, waiting for him to put on scrubs and latex gloves. When he reached for her, holding a scalpel in his hand, her eyes opened wide.

"Fix me my love. Make me whole again."

He woke up with the image of her face lingering in his mind, and instinctively knew what she had asked of him. "You'll always be in my life, my love. I'll be back."

* * *

He drove down the I-87 a bit after midnight. After two hours, he arrived downtown. The area by the Westside highway was deserted. He parked the car on the street and paced toward a building on Greenwich and West 11th St. The elevator took him to the third floor.

He hadn't been back to the apartment since her passing. After turning on the lights in the bedroom, he rushed to the wardrobe and shuffled through his clothes. He pulled a suit, and went to the bathroom where he spent a good ten minutes under the hot shower stream. He groomed his beard and hair, then sprayed a touch of perfume and put on his attire. A peek in the full-length mirror made him smile. The transformation was complete.

He returned to street level and hailed a cab.

"Greenwich and Spring," he instructed the driver. Upon arrival at his destination, he walked to the entrance of a night-club. The bouncer nodded, and let him in.

The inside was dim-lit. A row of people stood by the bar. He passed them without a glance. In the back, he saw a series of chairs and sofas with tables; girls and guys dancing to the deafening beat, occasionally sipping on their cocktails and beers.

He moved directly to the darkest corner and sat on one of the sofas, and after a few minutes, pretended to reach for a drink that was not his. He noticed one of the girls was smiling at him, batting her eyelashes. He smiled in return. When she bent over to talk to him, her hand brushed his knee.

"I think this is my drink," she shouted, pointing at the glass. The music was too loud. He smiled again and shrugged. "Sorry."

"That's ok. I'll get another one."

"No, no" he said, "mine", and pointed at the bar. "Wanna come with me?"

The girl grinned.

* * *

He had to keep the girl in the trunk on a bed of ice. He felt exhausted, but the excitement of what awaited him gave him the adrenaline he needed to drive back to the barn. When he pulled the girl out, her skin had turned slightly blue.

He walked to the shed and came back with some tools. The image of his beloved in his dreams never left his mind as he worked relentlessly, sweating through his blood-covered shirt.

* * *

He forced himself to stare at her. She looked nothing like she used to. Maggots had now started to devour her from the inside.

He succumbed to dreams again. This time, he saw a pond, hidden behind trees. She appeared before him, naked.

"Now that you've fixed me, you must do one more thing to bring me back," she said.

"What?" he responded with a broken voice.

She pointed at the water. "Feed me the cure."

He awoke to the stench of her rotting flesh.

The drive lasted a long time to the middle of nowhere.

* * *

He spooned her just like he used to after sex. He closed his eyes and waited. He didn't know how long it would take for her to shift, and started getting anxious about it. He held her hand in order to calm himself down.

When opening his eyes, he could not believe what he saw. Her teeth had sunken deep into his arm, frenetically feasting on his own flesh.

"You're back!" he exclaimed, ignoring the pain.

Tears of joy welled in his eyes. She looked at him and smiled with a blood-covered mouth.

"Yes, my love," she said, before ripping his head off.

Idle

A stale smell of sweat and blood lingered in the shop. Bill was busy cleaning his machine and preparing some needles for the next day. On Thursdays he always remained the last one working until close of business at two AM.

Over forty-five years old, Bill had been working as a tattoo artist for thirty years. Marking people with ink was his plight and his gift. He loved it, and hated it at times, depending on his mood and the design he was paid to create.

He glanced at the clock hanging above the entrance door. One-thirty AM already, and he still had to put away bottles of pigments and wipe his station, on top of taking care of this horrible vomit stain a much kindhearted customer had left in the bathroom earlier that day. As Bill took out the mop and started wiping the dirty floor tiles, he heard the doorbell chime. Did Jimmy the apprentice forget something and come back to pick it up?

When Bill exited the bathroom, he was surprised to see a stranger waiting by the desk at the entrance. The guy wore a black duster. His hair was very long, covering half of his face and dripping below his shoulders. His fingernails were painted in black.

Bill's eyes narrowed. He put the mop away, and made his move to the front of the shop.

"What can I do for you?" Bill asked.

"Hi. My band is touring in the area and our show just ended. I wanted to get a small something on my wrist."

The stranger pulled the sleeve of the duster to reveal the palest skin Bill had ever seen.

"Right here." He pointed with his index finger. The black nail landed on a spot right below his palm.

"You're not drunk, are you?" Bill asked. "Because I don't tattoo drunks. They never sit still and they always forget to pay."

The guy laughed. His voice echoed in an eerie manner inside the shop. "No. I'm not drunk," he replied, smiling without showing teeth.

"Just FYI, minimum payment is $100."

"Alright."

"So what do you want?"

"Well… I'm looking to see how good you say you are. I heard that you were quite talented and it piqued my curiosity. So let's start with something delicate first."

Both Bill's eyebrows rose simultaneously.

"It won't be long, I promise, and if I like your work, I'll come back for more. Heck, the whole band will come back for more!" the stranger said.

This statement was enough to convince Bill to start the tattoo. The design looked quite simple. It was a small black bird, its wings spread wide open, its feet pushed forward in the action of landing. No shading necessary; the tattoo would be solid black. Bill spent fifteen silent minutes on the piece and received the one hundred dollars in return.

"You're a good man, and you will be rewarded for your kindness. I shall see you soon, my friend." After saying these exact words, the stranger exited the shop. His duster muffled the sound of his steps on the street pavement, and he disappeared into the darkness.

Jimmy woke Bill up in the shop the next morning. When the boy poked the tattooist's arm, Bill jumped and almost slapped the youngster.

"Boss, you okay?" Jimmy asked.

"Damn!" Bill responded. "Do you believe that? I didn't even go home last night…"

"You left the door open too, Boss."

"Shit."

Bill moved Jimmy out of the way and went to the bathroom. When he looked at the tiles he noticed the vomit stain was gone. Good, so he had cleaned before falling asleep. After finishing his business, he returned to the desk and checked the cash in the safe. Nothing was missing.

"Boss…?" Jimmy asked, watching Bill.

"What's up?"

"Did you smoke weed last night?"

Bill didn't flinch. "Does it smell like weed to you?"

Jimmy shrugged. "I don't know, Boss. I just can't figure how you dozed off like that. It's not your style."

Bill stared at his apprentice. "And what's my style?"

"Well, Boss, you usually lock the shop door and fall asleep in your bed."

"Jimmy, I have no clue as to what happened. All I know is I cleaned the mess in the bathroom and then I was out."

"So nothing came up?"

"Like what?"

"I dunno. Something. Someone maybe drugged up your water?"

"You watch too many movies, kid. Go get your station ready. We have an appointment coming in thirty minutes."

"Ok," Jimmy frowned.

As the apprentice went to prepare his tools, Bill noticed the drawing of the black bird on the desk.

"Boss, you're gonna be okay working all day? I can cover your shift ya know," Jimmy said from his station.

Bill ignored the apprentice's question, too distracted by the bird he had no recollection tattooing. He showed the stencil to Jimmy.

"Did you do this yesterday?"

Jimmy shook his head. "Nope."

"Weird."

* * *

A whole other week passed. Business was slow, leaving the two tattooists idle in the shop. Most people wanted small pieces done in one session, and Bill longed for customers ready to unload a few thousands for a whole back or even better, a body suit.

During these financially difficult times, Bill tried not to think too much about money. He kept himself busy by working on flash designs inspired from magazines and books, designs he would later display on the walls of the shop.

The evening came, and at two AM it was time to close. Bill heard the familiar doorbell chime while bagging up some trash. He noticed the man in a duster standing by the desk, his long black hair covering half of his face. The pale bony fingers lay on top of the counter, black painted nails shining against the ceiling light.

"May I help you?" Bill asked.

"Hi. My band is touring in the area and our show just ended. I wanted to get a small something on my wrist," the stranger said.

The same exact scene replayed and the next day, Jimmy shook his boss awake. "Boss, what the heck? You did it again!"

Bill had no recollection of the night before. As he leaned by the desk, he found the stencil of the bird. "Jimmy!"

"What's up, Boss?"

"Did you design this?" he asked, handing the drawing to the apprentice.

"Boss, you asked me this question last week already. Nope. I didn't do this."

"Strange…"

"Yeah, last week. The same day I found you asleep on the chair with the door of the shop left unlocked."

How could Bill not remember anything from tattooing this peculiar bird onto anyone? The drawing looked simple enough to be executed in less than twenty minutes.

Another week passed, and when Thursday midnight came, Jimmy was ready to leave the shop for the night. "Boss, honestly, you gonna be okay tonight by yourself?"

"Why do you ask that?"

"I worry about you, Boss. It feels like something evil happens here when you're alone."

Bill shook his head. "There's nothing evil in this world I haven't already seen, kid. I'll be fine."

"I dunno, Boss. If I were you, I'd take off tonight."

"Thanks kid, I'll be alright."

"You sure, you don't need help? I'm great at sweeping."

Bill sighed. "If you insist."

Jimmy put himself in gear to clean. When walking to the outside dumpster, he noticed someone enter the shop.

The stranger wore a duster, his long black hair covering half of his face. Jimmy couldn't hear the conversation between Bill and the man. The apprentice hid in the dark, witnessing the same exact scene from the past few weeks.

When Jimmy returned inside the shop, he found Bill sitting in his chair, dozed off. "Boss, you did it again!"

Bill opened his eyes, startled. "What have I done again?"

"I have no idea what's going on here, Boss, but it's no good. It's no good." Jimmy felt agitated. He moved to the counter and found the stencil of the bird. "Boss, you just tattooed this bird on this man's wrist, don't you remember?" He threw the piece of paper onto Bill's lap.

"Who worked on this?" Bill asked.

"You did, Boss!"

Bill shook his head. "I can't recall anything, kid. I just can't."

A new week went by. Jimmy started feeling concerned about Bill. The two tattooists didn't do much talking during their idle moments, which happened often in between occasional appointments, yet the apprentice sensed that Bill wasn't his usual self.

When Thursday came, Jimmy felt the need to say something about the stranger and the bird Bill couldn't remember tattooing.

"So we have no idea who the guy is, huh?" the youngster ventured while putting away pigment bottles.

"What guy?" Bill was busy drawing.

"The long haired duster dude. He didn't even sign a waiver?"

"Nope. Guess I forgot to give him one."

"Maybe he took it with him when he left."

"Maybe."

"Are you worried, Boss?" Jimmy finished cleaning and moved toward the front desk.

"About what?"

"This guy. He looked so… strange." Jimmy leaned against the counter.

"You say so. I don't remember, kid." Bill's attention was focused on the lines of a big white tiger.

"Don't you think it's weird you can't recall anything, Boss?"

"I don't know, Jimmy."

"You should go home early tonight, Boss." The boy was trying to make eye contact but Bill didn't once look up.

"Why?"

"I have a feeling that this guy will come back." Jimmy followed the movement of Bill's hand as the tattooist applied finishing touches on the claws of the tiger.

"You keep talking about that man, kid. Stop pushing my buttons with your nonsense."

"Boss…"

"What?" Bill pinned the tiger stencil behind him on the wall.

"I've been working here long enough. I should be in charge of closing the shop," Jimmy said, while nervously tapping his foot on the floor.

"You know I can't leave you here alone if a customer shows up. You're not fully licensed yet," Bill said.

"So let's close early. Why wait until two AM every time?" Jimmy protested.

"Because closing early is bad for business, kid."

Jimmy didn't know what else to say to change Bill's mind.

"So let me stay with you," he finally mumbled.

"Fine. But stop talking about this guy, will you?"

Jimmy was growing anxious about seeing the stranger again. Every hour that passed, he looked at the clock, scared to hit the two AM deadline. Bill noticed the youngster's agitation, and became annoyed. At six PM, his patience level had reached its limits.

"Jimmy," he said, "Go home."

Jimmy stared at Bill like a deer caught in the headlights.

"Kid, you're driving me nuts, moving around like a frantic bug stuck behind a window pane." He sighed. "Just go before I yell at you. I'm serious."

Jimmy knew talking back would be a risky move. He had been working for Bill since he was eighteen, and their five years together had taught him one crucial thing about his mentor: "don't fuck around or you'll get your ass kicked so hard you won't be able to sit for a month".

Jimmy reluctantly packed his bag. "'night Boss. Be safe," he said when crossing the threshold.

"See you tomorrow, kid," Bill replied.

Jimmy left the shop but didn't walk home. Too eager to see the stranger again, he waited for the man with the duster to reappear. And at two AM, he did.

The same scene played out, and Bill fell asleep in his chair. As the stranger exited the shop, Jimmy started following him. He maintained a safe distance not to be seen, yet after a few minutes of walking, realized he had lost sight of his target.

"Shit!" Jimmy swore under his breath.

"You should have listened to your boss, Jimmy," a voice behind him said.

The apprentice froze in place.

"Why are you so scared?" A hand grabbed the boy's shoulder. Jimmy recognized the black painted fingernails, which caused him to panic and wet himself.

"Shhhh. Now look at you, being all frazzled like that," the stranger said.

"Why do you keep coming back?" Jimmy's words rushed out of his mouth faster than he could think.

"Boy, there are a lot of things you can't understand."

"Why do you keep getting the same tattoo?" Jimmy asked.

"Shhhh."

As the apprentice turned around to face the stranger, Jimmy caught sight of the pale wrist on which he saw the fresh tattoo of the bird glow in the darkness.

"What are you?" Jimmy was terrified.

"If only you knew..." the stranger laughed.

"Tell me," the apprentice begged.

"Now, now, young boy..." the stranger said. "If I tell you, you must die. Are you ready to die?"

"I know you're going to kill me anyway."

"Why do you say that?"

"Because you're evil."

The stranger laughed again. "You really think you know what evil is?" he licked his lips with his tongue, and Jimmy's mouth gapped in horror. That man's tongue was long and narrow like a lizard, and also glowed in the dark.

"Why are you getting the same tattoo?"

"If you insist," the stranger said with a nonchalant tone. "A long time ago - before you were born - I was human like you. I had a family who I cherished and loved a girl who I wanted to marry. Yadi yada, everything was perfect. But one day, I met a man, just like you met me. I was working as an apprentice in a tattoo shop and this man came every week, the same day at the exact same time, to get a tattoo on his wrist. The tattoo of a bird, its wings wide open, feet pushed forward in the action of landing.

"That man followed me home and faced me like I am facing you now. I asked him the same question; why do you keep getting the same tattoo over and over again? You know what he replied?"

Jimmy shook his head.

"Come on kid, think before I kill you."

"He couldn't keep a tattoo on his skin?" Jimmy ventured.

"You aren't as stupid as you look, but you're not quite there yet," the stranger said. "He told me he had met a stranger who looked just like I do, and that man had asked him whether he wanted to die. The kid's curiosity got the best of him. After he died, he became what I became."

"You're not making any sense," Jimmy said.

"It will make sense to you, I can assure you of this, once you reach the other side," the stranger said. "What we are doesn't matter, kid. Humans always want to find a purpose behind their creation because they think they are more important than everything else. But did you know your existence only represents a few seconds of life at the scale of the entire universe?" The man smirked. "Let me tell you this. This tattoo is what we are here to protect, and for that reason and that reason alone, we wander the world to get it over and over again, because our skin, just like your fragile little life, simply reflects the quick passing of... time."

"Are you a demon?" Jimmy asked.

"You're not listening to me. What we are doesn't matter, kid."

"But I don't want to die!"

"You know it's too late for that." The stranger pivoted closer to Jimmy's face, smiling, then, with a quick snap, grabbed the apprentice by the throat and broke his neck.

The following Thursday night, two AM, Bill had not heard from Jimmy for a week. The doorbell chimed, and a man in a duster, with long hair covering half of his face and black painted fingernails, entered the shop.

"May I help you?" Bill asked.

"Hi. My band is touring in the area and our show just ended. I wanted to get a small something on my wrist," the man said. He pulled the sleeve of the duster and pointed to the area right below his palm. "Right here."

"You're not drunk, are you? Because I don't tattoo drunks. They never sit still and they always forget to pay," Bill said.

"No. I'm not drunk."

"It's $100 minimum."

"Alright," the man put down a bill on the counter.

"So what do you want?" Bill asked.

"Well… I'm looking to see how good you say you are. I heard that you were quite talented and it piqued my curiosity. So let's start with something delicate first."

Bill raised an eyebrow.

"It won't be long, I promise, and if I like your work, I'll come back for more. Heck, the whole band will come back for more!" the stranger said.

"Okay, make yourself comfortable." Bill pointed at the chair.

No further words were exchanged. Bill worked on the skin, wiping the overflow of ink with a clean paper towel. The stranger saw the bird take life on his wrist, the spread out wings capturing a moment in mid-air between emptiness and solid ground.

Tattoos were strange. As a human, the man never thought of them as being limited in time, even if they faded and disappeared once the body that carried them died. But he never had to come back every single week to get the same tattoo done, forever. The sense of quasi-eternity he thought he owned by permanently marking his and others' skin had become so delicate. The choice of word was right. Humans always measured everything based on their existence alone, without ever thinking that they would someday be outlasted. That tattoo didn't withstand time; it represented time in its purest essence, as the weak and fragile moment a life took until completely vanishing into the idle form of death.

The man's role was to come back as the reminder that nothing lasts forever.

"You're a good man, and will be rewarded for your kindness. I shall see you soon, Boss," the stranger said while exiting the shop, his duster muffling the sound of his steps as he disappeared into the darkness.

Look at me

Look at me, and tell me what you see. Do you believe in the reunion of our flesh and blood, and do you pray every night for forgiveness when you fall asleep? I gave up on life already. I let you die in my arms, and said nothing.

I've always adored your smile, full of love and joy, memory of the glorious past that we shared before everything turned to hell. I never thought I'd tell you this someday, but you should know. The babies are gone too.

My life was bound to you, and to the children you gave me. Now that I lost all of you, what will I become?

I had a dream last night. I felt the smoothness of your skin against mine. Your hips welcomed my touch when I turned around to hold your beautiful face, and kissed you. I tasted your mouth. The more my hands ran onto your breasts, and down your waistline, the more I pulled you toward me. I loved you with every inch of my body, pressing myself deep inside you as you moaned louder with every breath.

You surrendered to me. I grabbed you from behind, my hands following the curves of your ass while I entered you everywhere. You let me do these things to you, and even begged for more. I called you my whore, and you claimed no one could replace you because you were so good at fucking me hard. I liked it, baby. I never wanted you to stop when you went down on me, and swallowed all the way. Your kisses transported me to heaven after you played these evil tricks with your tongue. Your talent would never be surpassed.

And now, what? I miss you.

Yet, this dream made me whole again. I woke up with my pants down to my ankles, thrusting into this shitty doll I bought before this whole mess happened. Nothing feels as good as a great pussy, but this had to do for now.

I hate to admit that I fell for such perversion. I long to touch you again… I must accept the fact that you're gone forever, and I belong to no one else. I guess I'll wait for my time to arrive, and until then, I'll have my fun.

****

I drank a lot yesterday. I caught the news via the old portable radio we kept in the basement. Federal and state authorities quarantined the whole island of Manhattan, and all the power's been cut. The military's in town. They forced everybody to stay inside. They say it won't be long before we can go out again. They even told us not to panic. Mostly we mustn't use tap water. Bloody journalists who don't know shit about anything, they think they can teach me a lesson now?

I broke the glass against the wall and cut my hand in the process. I got so angry when I heard them talk in their politically correct jargon that everything would be alright. I know they're merely waiting for everybody to die, and then they'll torch the whole place clean, as if nothing happened.

So what do I get to lose? Yesterday, life felt great. Today, I lost everything I cared about, even myself.

I want to fuck a real woman, and come in her face before I get killed too.

****

So babe, guess what? Do you remember Annie from upstairs? I've always admired that woman's ass, even when you were still amongst us. I recognize I also lusted to suck on her nice tits for the rest of the night. Well, I invited her to dinner – not that there was much to fancy on, but she has low expectations.

I don't really know what took a hold of me, maybe a demonic presence or the slow passing of my own sanity. I touched her in places where she told me to back off. I couldn't believe she did that, so I slapped her hard, and she fell.

No, her skull didn't crack open. I barely knocked her out. I took advantage of it though. I pulled her to the bedroom, and tied her to the headboard so she wouldn't flee when she woke up.

I love her pussy. I so love it. She tastes like sweet honey. I'll go to hell for cheating on you… but a man has needs, you know?

****

It's been days, and I spent my whole time with Annie. She feels really good. I reached a point where I finish and start again, because I can't stop. She drives me wild. I handle her like a piece of meat and pound her so deep…

Her face bothered me so I used the paper bag trick, and it worked wonders. All I want is her ass, not her ugly face. I taped a picture of you on the bag, so every time I fuck her, I actually fuck you. I'm such a genius. I won't go to hell now, right babe?

I'm happy.

I listened to the news again, very briefly, and they said that the virus had shifted from waterborne to airborne. I honestly don't know what it'll change for us. We're doomed either way.

****

Annie's dead. She coughed blood all over me and shortly thereafter, stopped breathing. Worst blowjob ever.

Damn, I miss you.

I had no idea what to do with her, and she started to smell, so I dumped her down the chute. She didn't fit through the hole as one piece, obviously. The bathroom is a mess, and you would hate to see this. Good thing that you're dead, huh?

Humor helps the mood. I worked on this bitch all day, packed her well and bam, she was out the door in no time.

Tired now. Am going to bed.

Love you.

****

Been coughing all day, my dick hurts, I'm angry and thirsty. No booze left.

****

What's up? I'm not going to make it, but we knew that already. I feel lonely. I wish my nurse were here to give me medicine. But where is she? Oh yeah... cold.

The rest of mankind must have spent the whole morning watching us. I laughed. Talk about solidarity. We became an object of amusement to entertain the world until a better reality show will oust us off the air. I'd better bask in my fifteen minutes of fame while I can, right?

This journey cast a new light on my purpose in life. No one wanted me to stick around apparently.

Where is God now, huh?

Do you remember when we moved to the City together? We rented that small studio apartment downtown by Wall Street, and we had little money. We spent what we earned on the household, but we didn't mind. In our dreams, we made it big. These times felt wonderful.

I recall watching you take a shower, your naked body under the water flow, your hands touching places I raved about since the first time I made love to you... I can picture it right in front of me.

I asked you to play for me, and you smiled. You put a finger in your mouth and you licked it real good. Ah babe. You looked so beautiful.

Once your hand reached your pussy, I started rubbing myself too.

What I loved the most about you was your confidence. You never feared anything. You tried out everything I suggested, and knew exactly what to do to please me.

These days are gone. I'm sitting on this chair, my head on fire, and my nose bleeding, ready to jump on the boat that'll take me to the other side. Maybe you can straddle me again in heaven.

I never used to believe in those things.

****

Look at me. I won't last much longer. That's when good porn comes in handy.

Thank whoever's up there for all the Playboys I kept in the closet. I overdosed before the fever knocked me out completely. I know I'm done.

Shit. Blood.

Last seconds before darkness. Babe, I hope you'll still love me when I'll join you. Don't be mad at me, ok? I know I did bad things, not only to Annie, but to a lot of other girls. I'd rather leave in peace than with a heavy heart, so I'll confess this to you.

Once you passed, I took care of the kids.
And
Fhgkljs
I
hjhfjhljlsjljlsjljs
ate
hhlhljlsipoispk;/lsnlkjdoiu
them
jjljljuodup/wnf/lqwkjodpq
too
jglfjopppssjppanlklksnlfn;pd'f'kdggknln;;;;l;;;…

....
....
....
....!

Commute

8:25 am. Same old routine I have to go through. And it is only Wednesday. Thank God there are only five days in a work week. Well, on a good week at least. I could not keep going like this if I knew I had to do this non-stop, until collapsing from sleep deprivation.

This truly sucks. I overslept and it is pouring. If the weather was nice I would not feel so beat today. I just realize I forgot my umbrella at home. No time to go back. On top of being yelled at for being late, I am going to be soaked when reaching the office. It is really one of those days I should have called in sick just to spend a little bit more time in bed. But what can I do, really? I have so many bills to pay.

Ok. Let's just go. Follow the flow, walk like a robot, down the steps and up to the turnstiles, swipe your card, make sure you go through the first time; I can already feel the feet of the person behind me pushing me forward, stepping in my heels, wanting me to go faster than I can. Give me a minute, for fuck sake! Here, I am through. Now, I have to dodge the people running to catch their train; I sometimes admire my skills. No, I will not take that one, even if I am running a bit late; I refuse to jam myself in an overcrowded car just because I think I can save two minutes.

Gosh, I hate this.

Here, the crowd has left, let's find a comfortable pace. I still want to be able to move quickly enough. What is wrong with these people who slow down for no reason in the middle of the platform? Let me go through! You can stop whenever you want, but hey, look behind you! I'm here, don't you see me?

Now I am being impatient. I really cannot stand this stress level. I need a vacation. I will plan to take a few days off next week. Yes, that is a good resolution. Here we go. I am happier now. I wish I could smile but am sure everybody around me will think I lost my mind, although, nobody looks at me. I don't even think they would care if I had a heart attack. They probably would let me die on the tracks and complain even more about how inefficient public transportation is.

This city will be the end of me. I fear that it will suck me dry until I realize it is too late to get out.

Positive thinking. The train is finally coming. In about twenty minutes, it will be all over. And tonight, it will be the same all over again.

I like to jump in the last car, because it is usually the least crowded. It is nice; this train is empty today. I like that. It won't be so bad after all. I will adjust the volume of the music in my earphones a little bit louder so I can truly enjoy the ride. I am ready.

Why are we not moving? It is taking really long for the doors to close… Wait, they are making an announcement. What? Due to an investigation in one of the stations, the express train will stay stuck here and we all have to move out? Well, it is one of these days I guess. I knew it. This empty train looked too good to be true.

Time to catch a different line - the local. Glorious. I am walking on the platform, trying to cut my way through the slow moving crowd. Come on! Don't check your phone now! What is the rush? There is not even a signal since we are underground. I swear, sometimes I wonder whether every human being comes with a functioning brain. Maybe some of them need a reboot. I believe most of them do actually.

Alright, let's do this all over again. Another train is coming. Not empty this time. Of course, since everyone will be taking this one. And I am running seriously late. I will have to play the elbows if I want to find a spot.

Deep breath.

I can feel bodies crushing against me. My personal space has been reduced to a mere half square foot, and this woman is trying to invade it a bit more by taking off her coat. What is she doing? Can't she see I am here? Hello? Am I invisible to you? She gives me the stupidest look when I stare at her, like I am the one in the wrong here. This is getting ridiculous. Stop shuffling through your purse! What do you need? Please, let me get it for you, at least, you won't force me to feel your butt rubbing against my leg every time you bend over.

I can't even hold onto the pole, all these hands grabbing it make me dizzy. I am going to fall over if the conductor brakes for no reason. Well, I will just land right on top of her, and then will give her the same look she gave me earlier. What? Why do YOU even exist? I mean, can't you just disintegrate yourself and give me some of your space so I can finally hold onto something and not stumble all over the place?

This is by far a horrible way to start my day. I want to shoot myself in the head right now. The train is running slow, so it is going to take an eternity to reach the first stop… I have a whole ride to go, buddy, so speed it up, will you?

I am going to play with my music. Put on a sweet tune and distract myself. If that woman moves again, I will shake her hard, I swear!

Why am I so angry? I shouldn't be. Last time I tried a relaxation class I almost lost it though. These things aren't good for me. I just need to leave this city, go away for a few days, enjoy the sun and a good night sleep…

We have come to a full stop. Oh, what is the matter now?

"Train traffic ahead of us, please be patient."

I have enough of trying to stay calm and relaxed! How do you want me to keep my cool when everything started off the wrong foot? And I am going to get in even later. That is really my luck. I cannot stand the yelling. Not today at least.

Everybody is waiting. Nobody is talking. I keep staring at the sea of shoes around me. I see flip flops. Pretty cute toes. I can't look at her; she is hidden behind this fat old man. I will imagine the toes are cuter than the face. And where did this guy find these boots? They make me think of contract killer boots, the ones you give a last look at when you pass out after he shot you twice in the heart and you lay like a dirty rag on the bathroom floor, covered in blood and shit. I watch too many movies. I know. Although this is New York City. Anything can happen.

Well, this is nice actually; there are so many interesting characters to observe. I like to make up crazy stories about them. It helps pass the time. Talking about time, we still haven't moved. It has been five good minutes.

I must learn how to be less impatient.

****

I have always wondered how hard it would be to fall asleep while standing. I don't think it is that hard, since it just happened to me. I don't know what took me over; it felt like the surrounding darkness brought me back to my room, and my comfortable bed, right there, I could feel the sheets under my back and the soft pillow supporting my head.

Hold on a second. The power went off. The lights are out, and we are stuck in the middle of a tunnel. How long have we been standing there? Why don't I hear a noise coming from the people around me?

Is everybody dead?

Too good to be true.

The ceiling lights are flickering and coming back on now. I must not have been out for very long, maybe a couple of minutes. I am not really surprised; I have not had a good night sleep in weeks. I work around the clock too much and it is taking a toll on me. I have to slow down, maybe just leave everything and move some place else, find me a nice cottage on the coast or something. Ok, I am not the type who could live in a cottage first of all, so why am I even thinking about it?

I am losing my mind. False. My sanity will vanish long before I have time to realize how crazy I have become.

That is funny. I have never seen before moss covering the walls of the tunnel. It looks like an inviting green pasture right outside the window of the car. I always knew that there was a lot of underground running water, and it makes sense that moss would grow here. I mean, I don't know anything about moss, or even plants in general. I live in New York City, where every being is confined to a concrete jungle and even bugs don't fly near, that is why every time I go abroad I come back looking like I got gang-banged by a fleet of rabid mosquitoes.

This is very puzzling. The more I look at it, the more moss seems to grow on the walls. Am I having hallucinations now? I knew I needed a day off. Too little sleep for too long can seriously mess with your mind.

Let's take a deep breath.

Nobody is moving, not even this annoying woman. I don't think that anyone started panicking yet either. This is surprising for a crowded car how calm people are. I am quite impressed at the self-control these individuals are exercising, compared to the frenetic manners they adopted this morning when rushing inside and pushing me like angry bulldozers.

I think I am getting claustrophobic. If at least the train was moving, I would feel a bit better about being stuck with all these people in such a small space. It is just getting too uncomfortable.

What time is it?

****

The lights went off for a long time this time. People start to complain; some of them are losing their cool. The muscles of my legs are cramping since I can't move and adopt a more comfortable position. I wish I had a seat right now. I am also sure I would fall asleep again if I was sitting down.

Here we all are together, sharing so much and so little at the same time. I can almost feel their breath on me. I smell their fragrance and the wetness of coats and umbrellas all around me. And condensation has formed on the windows. I can still see my reflection in one of them, my head above everybody else. I look so tired. It is awful.

Time has stopped.

I can't seem to forget the stress of this morning, the noise of the train braking on the tracks and the crowd pushing me inside the car. I start to feel hot in here. I need to take off my jacket, but there is not enough room to navigate. Well, maybe I can push my lady friend over there, and give her a taste of her own medicine.

That was glorious! I pushed her the same way she pushed me earlier and she couldn't stand it! I love these moments. It makes me happy to be alive just to enjoy that spectacle. Priceless.

I think I feel better now. Yes, at least I can breathe. I can still see the moss outside, and it seems very close… as if it is covering the windows. No, this isn't possible.

How can moss grow so fast?

I am going to keep watching because I want to make sure I am not dreaming here. This is unbelievable. One second I look, it is across the wall from us, and now…. No way! It is crawling its way inside the car, right through the doors.

Ok, someone slap me. Someone throw a bucket of ice water at me because I must be asleep. This isn't happening. No, it's not. Why isn't the car moving? Is there moss maybe stuck in the wheels and…

Fuck me. Am I being serious right now?

Close your eyes for a few seconds. You, stupid lady, shut up! I don't need to hear your whining. Everybody is going to be late. You are not the center of the world with your fat ass.

Relax. Breathe in, breathe out. Keep doing that until your pulse comes back to normal, because you cannot panic. Not now. If you lose it, then it is over.

Please, why is this baby crying? He was not before, so why now?

Somebody pinch me and take me out of this hell!

Bodies get closer to me. A stale stench lingers around. Funny, I didn't notice it before. Maybe it is coming from the tunnel since we have been stuck here for a very long time. Wait. The stench is getting stronger. Did somebody have an accident?

Oh no.

****

I could not believe it either, but there it is. The moss. It came right through, forcing the doors of the car wide open and making its way inside, covering everything; the floor, the poles, and unfortunate passengers who stood right there. It just crawled everywhere, like a green sea of invisible termites devouring everything on their way.

I am not dreaming. This is really happening. I already thought this day would be horrible, but I was far from thinking it would be my last on this earth. I didn't even have time to say goodbye. Oh what the heck! It doesn't matter now. I am going to rot here until some governmental official finds me and writes an impersonal letter to my mom to let her know how I ended.

Pathetic.

Life is so unfair.

I cannot escape, people keep pushing me but there is nowhere to run. We are all stuck here, and we know what is happening. I am not even sure if I am scared of dying. This is the first time I am really pondering whether I want to live actually.

This game is devious. No possibility of survival whatsoever. I couldn't even kill that woman with the hope of making it out of here in one piece. It would bring me nothing. Well, since we are all going to die, maybe I should try to choke her. I really despise her; she was so rude to me all along.

Yes, let's try.

Man, it is not easy to kill someone! This moss is being much more successful at it than I am.

I still managed to knock her out, and then broke her neck with the heel of my foot because she deserved to die before me. So little for her big fat ass.

Bitch.

This city took the best of me; my money, my time, my sleep, my sanity, and now my life. What do I get in return for all my sacrifices? I witness people dying, and I await my own fate - patiently - because there is nothing else to do. I just have to count down the seconds until the moss reaches me and sucks me dry.

You know what New York City?

I really hate your guts.

Silent Diary

December 12

Today's my birthday. It's been a hectic day, I've been running all over the place trying to find some supplies at the drugstore. I don't know exactly how I can still stand after not sleeping for three days straight. I hope that things will get better.

I miss you. I didn't even know what to think about us until it all happened. The first time I met you… Do you remember it too? It was the summer, and I stayed over at a friend's place. You had just returned from a trip abroad, and I got introduced to you that same night.

I saw it in your eyes right away… I knew you liked me. I liked you too, but was in the midst of this toxic relationship, and didn't know what to do with my life. So lost… I didn't care if you kept staring at me, wanting to talk to me. I didn't feel ready for this yet. It was too soon and I never could have cheated.

I thought about you a little, but wasn't obsessed with you. Not yet. I saw you a few weeks later for the second time at this party you had at your house. The weather was perfect and I can still remember the smell of alcohol floating in the air because we were all so drunk. Oh how I laughed. You wanted to drink so much, and yes, you did drink a lot. We were happy. I'll always dream about your smile.

Nothing really happened between us. No, we only played around, but we knew, we both knew, that we liked each other. When I saw you for the third time at this other party, I thought to myself, I really want to get to know that guy. He seems so nice. Yes, I liked you.

And do you remember that after that third time, we didn't see each other for one full year? I didn't totally forget about you but I knew I couldn't think about you too much because I had a lot on my plate. My relationship was going downhill. I didn't know how to hold on. I went through these weird phases where I felt happy and then totally depressed. My heart got broken more than once. I don't like to reminisce about that.

When we finally met again, I grabbed your face that night at the bar we were all at and landed a kiss right on your mouth, and stayed stuck to it until you pushed me back. You didn't know how to react. I wasn't single yet. You felt confused, and didn't want to do anything that could hurt both of us. I even apologized to you because I thought I had offended you somehow. You brushed this thought away, and took me by the hand outside. It was very cold. Winter had come. You held me against you and then we kissed again, for a long time this time. Beautiful… My heartbeat rushed like I was flying. I didn't want to let go. I wish time had stopped right this instant. After we parted ways, I simply replayed the whole scene in my mind, over and over again. I didn't know until then how much you had changed my life.

And now here we are. I can't sleep anymore. I can't eat anymore. I look like a ghost, so I've stopped checking my reflection in the mirror. Last time I took a shower must have been three days ago, right after it all happened. I cried, I cried so much that night. I rushed and ran, trying to find and fix you, to no avail. I looked at you and you didn't recognize me. I squeezed your hand because I wanted to feel your touch but you didn't react back. My heart sank and I thought I was going to end up dying here. Alone.

Is it really what love's all about? I thought I knew what it felt like, until now. I can't say I love you though, because nothing happened between us. We never dated. We never had sex. We just kissed and held hands like two lovebirds in kindergarten.

I don't know what to think anymore. My eyelids feel heavy, I need to rest but can't leave you now. I'll always be with you, that's how much I care.

December 13

It's been three hours after midnight and I must have slept about twenty minutes. My eyes are burning. My mouth feels dry and my hands are cold. What's happening to me? I tried to drink some juice but couldn't even swallow. I went outside to smoke a cigarette, that's another habit that came right back. I thought I was done for good. Apparently not. I'm holding up for you. I'm not giving up.

When I remember what I endured before I broke up, I didn't know I had it in me to sustain more stress. This room's so cold, and empty. Nobody knows I'm here. I've always wondered… What am I to you? We weren't even close friends. We started playing this game as soon as I threw myself at you and you responded in kind. It was nice, so nice, but in the end, where did it take us? We just kept fooling around and now I can't claim anything from you. I don't have your love, and your life's just fine without me. Do you really need me to be happy?

I'm confused, but can't stop thinking about you. You lit a fire back inside me and it's still burning. Will it ever subside?

You're driving me totally crazy. I have to sleep.

December 14

I keep thinking of you but now I want more. I remember the times when we touched each other and how much I longed for you. I dreamt of you, and spent sleepless nights trying to find a way to figure you out. But you refused, and always denied the passion between us. You sought to escape from all the pain you experienced because of all the crazy relationships you had been through. I don't care how hurt you were, I was hurt too. I wanted to mend myself with you, and wanted to have you just for a little while to feel alive again.

Instead, you decided to reject me, like a disease. You still liked me though. So we kept playing around, and thought it wouldn't hurt us. We were really stupid. You can't prevent love from happening, and you knew it I'm sure. But you played recklessly until one of us fell for the other. We tried to set rules but nothing mattered to you. Remembering all of this makes me angrier.

I keep thinking of you all the time, and feel like a zombie now. My mind's yours, my dreams are filled with images of your face and when I close my eyes, I picture myself hugging you tight against me and kissing you forever. I'm sweating just at the idea. My hands don't keep still, I must touch you but I can't, so I'll touch myself instead. Are you even aware of how insane you made me?

Your eyes, your beautiful eyes kept following me that night and I tried to convince you that we were meant for each other. But you rejected me once again. You argued that you weren't interested in a serious relationship at that point. Who talked about a serious relationship? I wanted to have you. Just one night. Just one. But no, you decided it wouldn't be right.

I hate this. I can't even talk to you right now. You don't care, I don't know, you left me by myself and now I have to solve this stupid puzzle all on my own. I hate love, I curse it so much because it brought me only pain. There was no soothing in trying to kiss you. I bit harder into a poisonous fruit that simply kills me, little by little. You gave me hope, you know. I really thought it could work out, but it was just a waste of time.

Now that I'm finally alone I realize what a fool I was.

December 15

I think you're damaged goods. There's no point in staying here while feeling sorry for myself. I have to go.

December 18

I missed you so much. I tried to forget about you but can't. I simply can't. I got mad because I hadn't slept in days and the combination of sleep deprivation and not eating led me to become mad at the entire world. You were always so sweet, and never hurt me.

I was crazy to think I could maybe get your attention and your love. After all, you made it clear from the start that you only wanted to flirt and I agreed to it. I agreed to it every time we played. And every night after leaving you, I dreamed of you and saw myself falling in love with you, but then the next morning, I knew it was a mistake. I knew it, I knew it deep down that it wouldn't do us any good to be together. We were both so broken. My previous relationship also destroyed me to a point of no return. I'm damaged so deep to the core, I don't even know whether I'll ever survive such trauma.

I care about you a lot… While I was away, your friends called but I didn't want to respond so I ignored them. Was it bad from me to do so? I'm sure you don't mind. I'm in no mood to be social. I hate myself for feeling this way. I really do. You know how much I want to be good to you.

It doesn't bring anything to dwell on the past.

I hope we can speak soon.

December 19

I need a bad boy in my life but when I find one, I get hurt, I get hurt so much it's impossible to breathe. I can't survive the pain of having to deal with violence and anger on a daily basis. I thought you were different, that's why I liked you. Was I right or wrong? I don't know. I don't know anything anymore. I made mistakes and regret them deeply. I fooled you too. You were an angel coming to save me from my doom and I just blew it. I'm sorry… I'm so sorry… Will you ever forgive me? I can't look at myself. When I do, I want to punch the mirror hard until my fists bleed.

December 20

Christmas is around the corner and I wish you were here to celebrate it with me. I feel lonely right now… I thought hard about everything that happened. I was so hopeful, I realize it, and my expectations were too ambitious for me to ever reach them. I sit in a corner and want to cry but no tears fall. My heart's dry and my head hurts; I clench my fists and bite through my fingers until I can't take the physical pain anymore, because I need to feel alive.

I can't believe what I've done to you. It seems that everything happened just like in a dream, and I want to wake up to make sure that we're ok. But I know we aren't. The romantic in me believes in eternal redemption; will I ever be forgiven? Angels have forsaken me to a deeper hell, and I keep falling while never hitting any hard bottom. My fear of landing and coming to my senses doesn't hurt as much as the fear of the unknown. I really think that I ruined all my chances of ever saving us. You can't speak back to me, and even if you could, I'm sure you wouldn't utter a word.

This is so sad when I think about it. We were destined to experience something much greater than this.

What can I do when I know that all hope's gone?

I miss you.

December 21

I saw this couple on the subway today and they looked so in love. It was sweet to watch them hug each other. They didn't display their affection too much, just enough for me to want to be that girl and for you to be that guy. He kept stroking her hair and touching her face as if she was the most precious thing in the entire world. I really wish it had been us.

Ah… I'm longing for you. And yet no response has come. When are you finally going to wake up and talk to me?

December 22

I got a phone call today. They're looking for me and wanted to ask some questions. I don't know what to do… Maybe I should just go away and disappear until everybody has forgotten about me. This is getting too hard. How am I going to keep up and stay strong? You aren't even there to support me anymore… So what do I have to lose?

It's horrible. I feel so ashamed I don't know what will happen when I'll finally tell the truth. I'm having nightmares.

I'm going to sleep here and pray for you.

December 23

I thought long and hard about it and don't believe I have to say anything. I've done nothing wrong! It was an accident. How can I lose everything if what happened was just an accident? I wish you were here to help me decide what to do now. I want to leave and take a train, maybe go to California. I'm really drained.

I remember the pain I felt when I was married. I thought I could survive all the yelling and screaming, but in the end, I couldn't take it anymore. My life was pointless before I met you. I went through the motions without ever feeling happy, and I convinced myself that my life was over at that point. But you came and showed me there was another way to find peace.

I kept fighting you at first, because I believed I recognized the patterns that I knew from before. Things were different with you though. You never meant to hurt me in any way. I projected my fear and all the doubt I had on you and I realize that. I was clumsy, and tried to justify my actions by shielding myself behind an armor of nonsense. You saw right through to me and never gave up. You actually showed me the love I never had, and your affection woke me up at night and made me search for you in my dreams.

When I reminisce about everything that happened, I know it was the right choice to leave him. He was toxic and would have destroyed me if I had stayed longer. He threatened me with a knife, you know? He really did. I felt so scared when he came toward me and shoved the blade under my throat, calling me names and threatening to kill me if I didn't do as he said. I felt so helpless.

These times are gone now. I have to deal with another burden yet, and it's slowly eating me from the inside. I wish I could hear your voice and see your smile to uplift my spirits. Nobody deserves what you're going through, and I'm really sorry if it's my entire fault.

December 24

Another dawn, another day. They all look the same to me now. I want to break free from the misery I'm in, but can't find any exit. Maybe you'll show me the way out. I made you your favorite cake today. Red velvet. I know how much you like it because it always tasted so sweet to you. Plus, red's the color of love.

I've also noticed how beautiful you looked to me. I made you an angel in my eyes. Yes, now everything's perfect. A little longer and you'll finally get back to life, and this, all thanks to my talent! I'm an artist. I resurrected you.

December 25

Merry Christmas, my love! Oh you should take a look at yourself… Pure perfection. I took the time to carve you a new smile, so you can finally grin at me. I've always loved your smile so much… Today I've also decided to make you officially mine. Ah! It felt so good. I'm not ashamed of what I did anymore. I deserve to be happy! After all the pain I endured with my husband… I'm glad he's gone. Why should he be worthy of my love after all? He was a liar, and a monster. He used his fists against me and made me feel weak. I had lost all self-esteem with him.

With you, however, it was a different story. I knew you wouldn't resist me very long. I remember how reluctant you were to be with me, but I finally convinced you, didn't I? Yes, I made the right decision. I'm glad I did what I did.

For the first time I know that I'll sleep well tonight. My anguish has slowly disappeared and is now replaced by these bursts of energy! I don't know what's happening, it almost feels like you brought me back to life too!

Be well, my love. I'll see you tomorrow.

December 26

I tasted the salt of my tears. I really tried everything to bring you back, but nothing worked. I fooled myself in believing that you loved me and you'd fight for me. In the end all hope's gone.

I'm leaving you today. I can't stay here any longer. They're looking for me. If they catch me, I'm dead. I can't risk this. I wish you could come with me on my new journey. I'll hold your hand a little longer. Adieu my love.

February 3

They caught me. They grabbed me like a rotten piece of garbage and threw me in this filthy hole in the middle of the ocean. I want to kill myself. They said I had done the unthinkable and deserved to stay here forever. I cried and screamed it was all an accident, but nobody wanted to listen. Why am I even talking about this? It's not like you care.

I'm so angry. They forced pills down my throat and told me I was sick. They also said I had psychological disorders. I can't control myself. I don't believe them. How could I have any disorder when everything that happened to you was a mere accident?

I remember that night like yesterday. I came over to your place and you had prepared dinner. We had a few drinks, and things heated up after that. I started kissing you, and we quickly wanted to do more so we went to the bedroom. Things were moving along perfectly, until you pushed me back and said you couldn't do it because I was confused after what happened with my marriage and you didn't want to hurt me. I became furious. I mean, who wouldn't?

You teased me and made me believe I could have you, and in the end, you rejected me. Again. I started going crazy. I grabbed the lamp from the bedside table and just kept hitting, and hitting, until I had no strength left. I think I fell asleep after that. When I woke up, you were at the same spot I left you the night before. Your face looked so peaceful. But you stopped talking to me. How unfair.

I wanted to apologize for what I did to you, and then you decided to keep your mouth shut. I was mad, but still wanted to keep an eye on you, so I stayed. And watched you. Every day, every night, I was there. Can't you tell it is love? Yes, I really loved you. You were so perfect to me. By the end, I thought you'd wake up and kiss me. You never did. It started smelling in the apartment and then they came. They stormed in and rummaged through everything. I don't know these people. Who were they? They violated our privacy.

I gave you a gift. I think your friends cried when they saw you. I thought my art was beautiful. Michelangelo beautiful. You'll smile forever now.

And I made you mine.

Never forget that.

Drop Dead Beautiful

Blood splattered everywhere. I pulled the trigger and didn't miss. One by one, I took them down.

They stood tall around me, marching like mangled paper dolls, wanting to kill, wanting to feed. I could smell the putrid essence of their brains oozing on their ragged clothes, bits eaten by time, devoured to the bone, white skulls and knuckles showing under atrophied muscles.

I never thought humanity could cease to exist until that day. I heard the clock chime three times and woke up to a growl. When I looked to my left, she was drooling at me, her eyes gouging out of their sockets, her cheeks scratched until she had pierced a hole with her nails in one of them, and her teeth kept snapping, fast and aggressive. She grabbed my arm and tried to bite, but I punched her in the nose instead, breaking the septum, sending shards of bones directly inside her forehead. I thought the injury would kill her, but it didn't even slow her down. She chased me inside the house, her feet sliding against the cold tiles of the kitchen floor, extending her hands like a child who saw something it desperately wanted. A guttural moan erupted from her mouth, and she opened wide, imitating chewing motions without chewing anything... yet. Her body adopted an awkward stance, her back arched ninety degrees forward, her spine almost breaking, her legs straight as two sticks, the knees locked in place, impossible to bend. She advanced and progressed on her journey toward me while I searched for an adequate weapon to quickly seal her fate and save myself.

I heard her growl behind me and browsed through the cupboards, looking for a wooden spoon or a sharp long kitchen knife, something I could stab her in the eye with, something I could cut her head with. I didn't care if she was my wife anymore. To me my wife was already dead.

2006. I enrolled in the military shortly after that incident. They were looking for volunteers to constitute Sweep Teams and help get rid of the vermin that kept colonizing earth. Dead bodies crawling from the ground, seeking to share space with the livings, desiring to become more than just dust, begging God for a purpose, a new chance to make things right. I personally had lost all incentive to find happiness after what I experienced with Lucy in our kitchen. I had only one goal in mind: kill all of them.

The Great Invasion had decimated a lot of our troops. I was one of the few with enough experience to train the new recruits and also complete suicide missions around the globe. Colonel Jackson congratulated me every time I came back alive, shaking my hand and looking at me with eyes that spoke more than what his mouth dared to say. I didn't give much credit to countless medals and decorations; to me, they belonged behind a clean window pane in a museum, not on my jacket.

The Dark Western Territories were considered a deadly zone. Nobody dreamt of going there as much as I did. I knew that the fiercest bodies gathered and fought humans until no flesh was left on their trembling skeletons.

Colonel Jackson talked about the bodies to be intelligent enough to have a leader. A female sneaked in and used unexpected strategies to attack and defeat entire battalions. I thought this was a myth. Dead bodies couldn't behave like us. Their brains didn't function the same way as ours.

I volunteered to go, despite the Colonel's warnings. I knew he liked me, and wanted to keep me alive to contain the spread of bodies across the country. Meanwhile, I needed to see their blood splash over my face while I chopped their heads off with my sword, one of the finest katanas I had stolen at the Museum of Asian Arts during the great pandemic that killed the whole population of Manhattan.

That blade could cut through steel. Sharp and precise. My weapon of choice when I faced them at gun point, finishing the job I started by shooting through their hearts to slow them down first. I also loved my Magnum. Big and loud, with bullets that formed craters inside their chests, large and wide; the ribcage expanded and the useless lungs dangled into thin air. A delightful spectacle indeed.

The bodies made me who I was. A thirsty killer, a sick mind that could never be healed, haunted by nightmares so violent I needed drugs to sleep my mandatory three hours every night. I hated them so much. I was used to vomit the acid that sat on my stomach after days of not eating. I drank Whiskey to keep going, the alcohol giving me the energy to stand, think and fight, the adrenaline bursting through my veins with every kill I scored, bringing me closer to my fate and my salvation.

I'd die once they all died. That was what I promised myself in tribute to Lucy.

Nobody clearly knew how the first one got infected. It happened overnight, or so it seemed. One day the world was fine; the next, it had become hell. A virus, waterborne then shifted airborne, took control of the children's minds first. Babies suckling onto their mother's breasts soon devoured the delicate flesh without mercy. Toddlers who watched their parents sleep soon nibbled on their lifeless fingers like juicy lollipops. The cycle of life had revolved backwards. Civilization slowly drowned in a pool of toothless mouths that had transformed into powerful jaws. All they did was eat. The adults who survived mutated into soulless killing machines. Lucy worked with kids; she loved being a teacher. And that was also the end of life as I knew it.

I couldn't bring myself to accept what had fallen upon us. My defense mechanism revealed itself to me, and I accepted my new condition without resistance. I relentlessly moved from battle to battle and drew the bodies' blood, their soiled remains filling my dreams, making me hard almost… I had lost my humanity yet I was still human. They were monstrosities that escaped the gates of a forgotten territory, a faraway land where the dead stayed among themselves and never left. They were meant to remain there. Forever.

I sent my request to be transferred to the Dark Western Territories to be effective immediately. Colonel Jackson objected, but I showed him how determined I was, and he signed it. A few hours later, I boarded a plane that landed in what I described a gigantic grave swarming with severed limbs and corpses that moved, walked and growled like an army of famished and bloodthirsty hounds. How long would they sustain their temporary state?

As long as they had living flesh to feed from.

****

I reached the base early and met with the individuals responsible for the Sweep Team. Five of them, all younger than me, certainly less experienced, but ready to follow, whatever it took, we had a mission and had to complete it. I didn't care how many bullets we would need, or how much gas we would burn, I wanted them all, collecting their heads like trophies I could display on my wall, maybe smoking a cigar and enjoying a glass of a sixteen year old scotch in a fancy crystal glass afterwards. Ideas. Fantasies. Nothing seemed to be real but the gruesome image of their mouths growling at me, their hands searching for my heart, ripping my skin with their bony fingers, drinking my blood like a juicy cocktail, and killing me, licking my eyeballs until I turned blind. I wanted them all. I wanted to slay until I couldn't stand anymore.

I held a momentary debriefing session with the guys, asked whether they had questions. Nobody dared to raise an arm. So I answered any concern they might have had, and if they were too ignorant not to stop me then, they would make perfect bait for our lovely criminals who already waited for us a few hundred miles outside. It felt as if they could almost sense my presence, and I could smell their stench. I was salivating at the thought of fighting them. My glory, my victory, my quest would finally find a purpose. I was ready to welcome them in my realm of horror.

My alarm was set for four hundred. A helicopter flew us to the drop zone, and would pick up the survivors twelve hours later. The objective was to find the leader of the bodies and destroy it. Her. She used to be a woman, now a hungry animal.

Like Lucy.

I brushed the memory away as I looked outside. The soil seemed frozen in time, grass stopped growing, nature surrendered to the evil populating the ground, because witnessing their evolution was too much. It felt like too much for me already. I gulped some Whiskey to boost my energy. A few drops fell at my feet, and I imagined them being blood. Distorted visions invaded my mind, my body moving like a robot, my open mouth screaming as if screams intimidated them. I laughed. Nothing intimidated them. They didn't know fear. They didn't know anything.

Only hunger.

I couldn't fathom the future of this world with them as the superior species. Why did God choose to forsake us? I believed there was a God before everything collapsed under my feet. My life vanished from my eyes and got replaced with pain, my heart aching to a point where I couldn't feel anymore. I lost her. I lost myself. I lost faith in everything. Saving whoever could be saved wouldn't be considered a miracle. Merely a postponement of what awaited them next. More horror. More pain. And death as a result, only to become a walking hungry demon looming to feed from the remaining souls still wandering in the open until everything was gone. What a waste.

Talk about heaven. I had no idea where to find it. I gulped more Whiskey. The helicopter was approaching the drop zone. I prepared my chute, ready to descend among them. I couldn't see any body near, maybe they were hiding somewhere, expecting us to come to them. Sly arrogant bastards. I despised them all. Wanted them dead for good.

I jumped and let the weight of my body drag me to the hard landing bottom. The chute pulled me higher when it opened, giving me the opportunity to survey the land one last time. Empty. Deserted. I knew they waited in the darkness. I could sense them. My eyes pierced through the fog and tried to find them. But silence and solitude welcomed me home instead.

I glanced to my left and right. My guys all stood next to me.

"Let's go get them!" I shouted and they followed me without protesting.

My body moved but my mind stayed still. I watched Lucy's head fall down my lap when I shoved the wooden spoon right inside her right socket and she looked at me from her left eye, still snapping at my face, her bloody fingers grabbing my shirt, tearing the fabric apart, scratching me, leaving dirty marks on the skin of my stomach. I couldn't watch her, so I closed my eyes, and grabbed a handful of hair while I pressed the blade of a carving knife against her swollen throat. I started cutting, pushing her mouth away from me, holding her head still, she growled, growled some more, her bloody gurgles flooding every one of my thoughts, I cut, cut, cut, always deeper, until the head detached itself from her mangled body. When I finally opened my eyes, a distorted face grimaced at me, a wooden spoon stuck in the right socket. My Lucy had turned into a monster. I sat in a pool of her blood. I believed I would get infected. But for some deranged ungodly reason, I didn't.

The cold air kissed my cheeks, and I pulled my Magnum. I knew the bodies hid not far from us.

"Come out! Come out!" I yelled as loud as I could. My guys covered my flanks.

I advanced in direction of the woods. The bodies loved the woods. Gave them an advantage over us. But I wouldn't enter. I wanted them to see me and come get me. The bodies were stupid. No way they could think like us. I didn't believe they even had a leader.

I moved further north. Gestured to my men to spread. Six of us against hundreds of them. Colonel Jackson might have been right for once. I should have stayed away. This mission was by far the most dangerous I had ever attempted.

I briefly stopped and listened. A growl. I had heard a growl. I glanced around. A shape. Running. I locked my aim and shot. The body fell. Another shape. Coming from my right. One of my guys popped a bullet and the head exploded like a pumpkin.

More appeared. I put myself into fight mode. I forgot the past and focused on the present task. I let them exit the woods and march toward me.

My babies were looking for their mama.

I forgot about time. Hours passed and I reloaded my gun, stalling them long enough to pull my katana and cut them in halves, exposing their rotten debris to the world. They moved like paper dolls, so strong and so weak, staring at me with their broken faces, howling at me, searching for my heart in the darkness. I shot, then sliced, shot again and stabbed, dancing among the cadavers, drunk and delirious. My laughter filled the space between them and me, and I ran and dodged, ducked and jumped. I was a super hero. Invincible.

Her smile broke my bliss and brought me back to reality. Lucy. My drop dead beautiful wife lay next to me.

"I thought you were dead…" I whispered while holding her silky silhouette.

"Here I am, my love. Forever by your side."

Tears welled in my eyes, sudden sadness melting me like ice, and I searched for her warmth, longing for her smell, her touch, her lips, her hair. I couldn't stand being far from her. She was mine. She should have stayed with me.

"Why did you leave?" I asked, crying.

"You killed me, remember?"

"I had no choice." I begged. "Forgive me."

"You could have become one of us. One of them."

"Never."

"You should never say never, my love."

Her mouth moved closer to mine and I let her kiss me, losing myself in her embrace.

She should have stayed with me, I repeated in my head.

A loud and deafening growl pulled me out of my funk. The ground of the forest felt so cold to the touch. Blood kept pounding inside my head. I didn't realize I had fallen under. For how long? I tried to find my guys, but saw nobody.

Was I the last one alive?

A shape moved toward me. A woman. My blurred vision played tricks on my mind. Lucy?

"How did you come here?" I asked while the shape came closer.

The creature growled. She looked exactly like her. Same height, same petite frame, same dark long curly hair, same eyes... Dark blue, shining as bright as two sapphires. Lucy...

I searched for my gun. My Magnum. Where was it? I couldn't look away from her. My katana. Still on my hip.

I grabbed the weapon and slowly stood up, always facing her. She had stopped walking. Her hands at her sides, she remained perfectly still.

I waved the blade at her.

"I killed you once! I can kill you twice!" I said.

She growled. She curled her lips and revealed bloody teeth filed like sharp pointy razorblades. She pulled her tongue out, black and blue, and licked them very slowly. I felt paralyzed, hypnotized by her. She knew exactly what she was doing, choosing every move precisely, taking her time, savoring me as her next victim. Sweat beaded on my forehead.

Whiskey. I needed to drink. I patted my jacket pockets and found the flask. Without losing sight of her, I untwisted the cap with my teeth and finished what was left of the precious liquor. The taste immediately reinvigorated me, running down my throat, bringing warmth back to my core. I tossed the flask away.

She growled again. I prepared to inflict a lethal blow.

"What are you waiting for?" I provoked her.

She started shifting her weight from one foot to the other, her arms rising as if she wanted to take a long jump. But the distance between us was too small for her to attempt anything of the sort. I felt confused. She didn't seem as disarticulated at the other bodies I slaughtered. I even thought I caught a glimpse of intelligence in her dead eyes. It was impossible. She couldn't think like me. No, she couldn't.

I decided to move first. I only had to hit her once. Right on the neck.

My field of vision narrowed, focusing only on her. I had no idea if other bodies stood behind me. I was maybe surrounded by hundreds of them. I wanted her. Their leader. My Lucy look-alike. She would be mine again.

I screamed and lunged toward her. My mouth opened, my eyes bulging out of their sockets, I could almost picture my body attacking her in slow motion while she stayed in the same position. I lowered the blade and aimed at her throat. I had come so close. My triumph. My deliverance. My final escape.

****

I felt a void inside my head, as if some surgeon had opened my skull and scooped half of my brains out with a teaspoon. It didn't really hurt. I experienced quite a comfortable feeling, a sort of light numbness similar to the beginning stages of drunkenness.

I recognized in a blur the silhouette of a body next to me. I tried to move out of bed, but couldn't, somehow fully paralyzed from neck down. I heard a clicking sound, something my teeth would normally do when I reached a lower body temperature. The room felt actually very hot, almost steamy.

I stayed there for a while, not really sure what to do. I still couldn't see clearly. When I pressed my lips together, I realized my mouth was utterly dry. I needed to drink water.

Something snapped. It crawled from behind my neck, slowly nibbling on my ear, and ran down my chest. Its million legs stuck onto my skin, each part of his umbilical skeleton cracking with every move, leaving me powerless, unable to scream. My tongue had disappeared, leaving an immense gap inside my throat. I shivered although it was too hot for me to be cold. And I wasn't afraid.

The million-legged creature continued its journey onto my stomach until it found my navel. I finally recognized its shape as it paused, raising itself into a perfect vertical stick. It looked like a big caterpillar, reinforced with a thick carapace. The bug remained rigid for a long time, while I kept staring at it, not really sure of what it might do to me. I was still out of it.

The stick held its position until I got too tired of watching. As I put my head back against the pillow, I drifted into a deep daydream.

I saw myself walk across the battlefield, my weapon in my hand, obliterating them like paper dolls. Blood spilled everywhere, and I heard their screams as they fell onto the ground, eaten by death, but never gone for too long anyway. I popped bullets into their brains, fighting until I was the last one standing.

I didn't win, did I?

The caterpillar still stood above my navel when I slightly opened my eyes. A familiar sensation invaded my body.

Then I smelt it. The rancid odor of blood covering my skin hit my nostrils harder than if an entire bottle of fragrance had shattered on the floor. My mouth immediately salivated.

The paralysis subsided, and so did everything else. All that remained was this insatiable hunger.

I needed to feed, now.

Canceled

A bloody handprint smeared the mirror. I stared at my reflection and slowly traced the words "Fuck you" with my index finger.

****

Halloween. I had planned the whole night for weeks. I wanted to go to this party downtown, and invited him. Ethan. Not my boyfriend, not my friend, just a guy I had met a few months earlier and with whom shared my lonely nights. I didn't know what to expect. A dumb girlfriend's advice forced me to make him more than what he was. Silly.

The evening started weird.

"So you'd rather be with your friends than with me. I get it. Somebody lost some cool points in my book. Whatever. I'll call you once I'm done. Bye."

I hung up on him and let out a shriek of frustration. After tossing the phone on the couch, I grabbed the bottle of Black Label and poured myself a couple of drinks. I closed my eyes and let the liquor run down my throat. I always met Ethan at his tiny one bedroom apartment. Nothing fancy, nothing romantic, just bestial sex we both craved. I didn't mind the age difference because it actually made the whole game easier. No strings attached meant no feelings involved and only the immediate satisfaction of primal needs.

Laura was wrong. I didn't like him and didn't need him in my life to be happier. Ethan served one purpose. Why did I listen to my girlfriend's ramblings when she tried to persuade me I was infatuated with him? Dumb. I chugged the rest of my scotch and sat on the chair. My phone blinked.

"Hello? What? You know, it's actually a great idea. I'll see you there."

My other friend Colette told me she had drugs and I got excited. Getting high would help me ease the tension after the stupid exchange with Ethan. Guys pissed me off. I wanted to forget about him.

After turning up the volume on the TV, I applied my make-up and morphed into the disco queen I intended to be. I added lots of glitter, black shiny pants, high heel boots, and tied my hair into a big puffy bun. From up close I looked like a hooker, but acting trashy on Halloween was recommended so I wouldn't stand out.

It had snowed all afternoon, and the City had lost all its energy as people left the outside to stay inside. I must have been one of the few lunatics who decided to go out that night.

I was welcomed by slush and rain. I pulled up the hood of my coat and paced to reach Second Avenue to hail a cab. It took less than five minutes to find one. Easy enough. I closed the door behind me with wet fingers and gave the driver the address. West Houston and Seventh Avenue, a bar called "Blue". All my friends were gathered there and we would have plenty of fun.

During the ride, I lost myself glancing at my phone to check whether a text message from Ethan had come. Maybe he'd show up afterwards, surprise me, make me believe he was different from the selfish prick I considered him to be. Of course, nothing came.

****

The bouncer at the entrance checked my ID, and I entered Blue. A thick crowd stood in my way and I pushed people to cut through. My heels helped give me the extra inches I needed to search for Laura and Colette above all the heads. I noticed the bartender. He had dressed up like a zombie – how original – and smeared his face with fake blood. His eyes looked completely white, the iris included. His two black pinhole pupils followed my every movement as I leaned against the edge of the bar. Where the heck were my friends? These bitches didn't even text me to tell me they were on their way. I grew impatient and played with my phone, waiting for one of them to get in touch with me.

A hand grabbed my forearm and cold fingers scratched my skin.

"Ouch!" I said, noticing the fingers belonged to the bartender.

By the way he was staring at me, I freaked out and pulled my arm away from his reach, rubbing the area where he had held me.

What the fuck?

The bastard had left scarlet marks all over my skin, as if he had attacked me with an ice pick or something. Great. Now on top of not finding my friends, I was bleeding. I needed a tissue and alcohol to disinfect the tiny wounds. I scowled and ordered a shot of Everclear.

"We don't have that here, milady." He smirked and bared his teeth.

What a jerk.

"Then give me a shot of the strongest alcohol you have," I replied with an angry tone.

He didn't respond and walked away from the bar, leaving me time to scout for my friends again. I really had no idea where to find them. The marks on my arm burned and I wanted to scratch, but stopped myself and played with my phone instead. There was no message from anyone. I wondered whether they would ever show up.

The glass landed in front me faster than I had expected. The bartender smiled again, bearing the stupidest look on his face, and I wish I could have slapped him when I had the chance after he hurt me. I was beyond pissed. I gave him the exact change, no tip, and dipped my fingers into the shot glass before applying the pure alcohol onto my injured arm. The liquor helped me feel more at peace with the idea of catching a disease from this psycho bartender.

I gulped the rest of the alcohol and stepped away from the bar, trying to blend in with the crowd. Despite the high number of people, the air felt terribly cold and my breath clouded in front of me. I wanted to pee, check the bathroom, wash my hands and maybe score some drugs while I waited for the girls to show up. I hated when people were late.

I moved further to the back but it took me a while to finally locate the ladies room sign. I reached the first open stall and locked the door behind me, and after I finished my business, decided to make a call to check where everyone was.

Ring. Ring. Ring. Ring. Ring.

"Hi, you've reached Laura Bendman. I'm not available at the moment. Please leave a message and I'll get back to you as soon as I can. Thank you!"

Beep.

"Hey! I'm at Blue. Where are you?"

I didn't leave my name. Crap. Whatever. She would know it was me, and the bitch could seriously beat it after standing me up.

I tried Colette.

Ring. Ring. Ring. Ring. Ring.

"Hi, it's Colette…"

Christ! Nobody picked up! I must have called every contact in my phone and no one, absolutely no one, answered. I honestly had enough of this shit. I didn't even want to stick around. Were they playing a joke on me?

Because I hated this whole plan. I should have been wiser and stayed home with a bottle of wine. Maybe Ethan would have come later and we could have spent some sweet time together…

Thump.

A bang on the door. Hold on a second. No. It couldn't be.

Thump.

Another one. Harder this time. What the fuck was wrong with everyone tonight?

THUMP.

"Go away!" I yelled. "I'm busy! There's no one next door."

THUMP!

Now whoever stood behind that door hit it so hard, I seriously thought it had come off its hinges. Another loud bang and the door would crash on my head.

"FUCK OFF!" I screamed so hard I almost lost my voice.

It was dark inside the stall, and I felt cold, even colder than before, but didn't want to open the door and get punched in the face or something. I didn't like this place at all! Then the alcohol hit me. Numbness invaded my head, my vision slightly blurred, and my level of frustration maxed out immediately. Whoever stood behind that fucking joke of a door would have a difficult time reasoning with me. Back on my feet, I relaxed my back, even cracked my knuckles and clenched my fists. I was on fire tonight!

THUMP!!

"Oh fuck you!!! I'm coming out now. On the count of three. One… Two…"

As I went to remove the lock, fingers grabbed the door from the other side, and my heart stopped beating for a second. Nothing made sense. All my courage instantly left me, and I felt frozen, unable to make a decision, and unable to comprehend whatever was happening outside the stall.

I swallowed very slowly and tried to stay calm.

"Alright. Whoever had the brilliant idea to scare me, it didn't work. So I'm coming out now, and you better get the fuck away from me!"

I thought I yelled but didn't know how loud because more fingers held stronger to the door and shook it really hard, trying to break it open. I looked up and down and more fingers appeared. How many were there, maybe five, maybe ten different pairs of hands fighting to open the only barrier sheltering me from them? I didn't know what to do anymore. My screaming clearly didn't intimidate anyone.

My mushy thoughts stalled inside the fog that became of my head and the hands multiplied. Why did I have to drink so many shots of hard liquor beforehand? The more I looked, the more the entire frame of the door was covered with a blackish residue. I rubbed my eyes and tried to calm myself. I was drunk. I was imagining things. As a last resort to give me peace of mind, I grabbed my phone and used its light to tell what the substance was… Oh my god!!!!! It looked like blood. Real, fake, I didn't care at that point and climbed on top of the toilet.

"If this is a joke, you're freaking retarded. Laura, is that you?" I screamed again, now convinced my voice sounded more like a whisper. The hands gripped onto the door so hard they almost managed to take it off the hinges. Thirty more seconds and I was done.

I started breathing hard, so hard I hyperventilated. This wasn't real. It couldn't be. In a last desperate attempt, I glanced around and took mental notes of my environment but realized my possibilities of an alternate escape route didn't exist. My heart rate increased so much I couldn't inhale anymore. I choked and then felt vomit in my mouth. I retched, coughed, retched again, and then finally… Ew! I threw up all over my shirt. At least I felt less drunk but it didn't change the fact I couldn't get away. The vomit started to smell so badly I wanted to puke again. God, when would the horror end? I stopped myself from retching, and stared at the door.

I needed to at least know what awaited me outside the stall, so I used my phone to take pictures from above with the flash, and snapped about ten times before browsing through the shots.

I gasped. Blood. Everywhere. Across their faces and bodies... One of them was missing an arm. Another had an empty eye socket. Oh God, was it just more than make-up?

I swallowed hard but all I tasted was my own vomit. FUCK!!!!!! The noise of the door breaking off the hinges was driving me crazy.

"Make it stop already!" I screamed, and when I looked at my phone, a teardrop splashed on the screen.

****

I rang the doorbell.

"Who is it?" I heard through the intercom.

"It's me. Open," I replied with a rather disembodied voice.

"Who me?"

"Don't play smartass. Just open."

The loud buzz told me I could go in. I followed the motions without thinking about them, and walked up the stairs, four flights, until I reached his door. Apartment 5E. He had left it unlocked. What a dumbass. I twisted the knob. Slowly. The door squeaked and I entered. I didn't bother to lock after me. No need to worry about that because I had a more important task ahead.

I walked down the hallway leading to his room. As I let my fingers run freely on the white wall, an evil laughter rose from my broken jaw. I felt good. I felt high. I wanted him to console me, hold me tight while we fucked hard, him pounding inside me like the true whore he thought I was. Except tonight, I wasn't a whore anymore.

He lay on top of the bed with his pajamas on, his eyes already shut to sleep.

"Wake up!" I ordered with a growl.

"I'm wasted and tired. You'll have to do all the work tonight," he slurred.

I moved closer to him and scratched his cheek.

"You want me to fuck you? Is that what you want?" I pressed a finger against the skin of his neck and felt his pulse.

"I don't care." He pushed my hand away and turned on his side, showing me his back.

I laughed again while I took off my coat. The garment dropped on the hardwood floor, followed by my pants and vomit soaked top, leaving me with only my shoes and underwear. I walked around the bed several times, never losing sight of him. Ethan, my dear Ethan...

"You should take off your heels or the neighbors will complain," he mumbled.

Oh Ethan, if only you knew how I didn't give a fuck about your neighbors.

I climbed on top of the bed and positioned him on his back. I sat on top of him, my legs on each side, and caressed his arms. He was gone; I listened to his breathing.

I parted his lips and inserted my tongue inside his mouth. He quickly responded in kind, and I rubbed myself against him, my hand not leaving his crotch while my kiss grew more passionate. His warmth filled me in. My hair dripped on his face, and my legs pressed on his sides. My fingers explored him, exciting him more and more as I stroked him. He liked what I did to him. He always told me I possessed great skills.

He soon was turned on enough for me to remove my panties, and I gently straddled him, feeling him slide inside me. My cold body suddenly became a hot mess. He placed his hands on my hips to give me the needed cadence to ride him right, alternating hard and soft, my upper body rising into a vertical position when I finally climaxed. I didn't stop kissing him and slowly pulled myself off him to finish him with my mouth instead. My lips ran down his sculpted chest, his six-pack abs and his perfect waist. The motherfucker had a killer body and I spent a long time playing with my tongue on his skin, tickling him.

The more I sucked, the more he moaned. His hands grabbed my hair and he moved my head up and down, up and down, moaning, moaning louder, I kept pulling him inside my mouth, swallowing him whole, forcing him to release and scream. He tasted delicious, like sweet and sour candy.

His hands dropped on each side of his body when he exhaled his last breath. I left the bed and walked to the bathroom. I felt a bit disoriented, my legs dragging under me. I turned on the light and stared in the mirror.

Besides my mangled jaw, a yellow substance also oozed from scratches on my face. I moved closer and looked at my eyes. The irises had turned white like the rest of the eyeball, and my pupils were two empty dark pinholes.

I laughed again and my bloody fingers slammed the glass.

****

The door finally gave up and I found them longing for me. Their cold embrace devoured my flesh, and males and females chewed and fucked me at the same time, my muffled cries lost among the snarls that rose from the bathroom stall. They ripped my clothes off, bit my nipples and fingered my mouth. I could feel them everywhere… I was being loved like the true whore Ethan told me I was, Ethan, my lovely booty call who never gave a fuck about me. I let them impale me all at once, and I enjoyed it. I never thought I could experience something like this. I didn't need drugs, I didn't need booze, because the depraved undead sex gave me all I ever wanted.

I liked you Ethan. I couldn't wait for you to fuck me like that, break me in halves and eat my insides until I fainted. You were such an asshole ignoring my calls, but it didn't matter anymore what you did and didn't do to me.

After that Halloween night, your amateurish show was definitely canceled.

About the Author:

As a kid, I dreamt of becoming a writer. I finished my first novel at the age of nine and authored poems and more stories for many years after that, including two movie scripts at seventeen. My crazy dreams wanted to take me to the movie industry, where I would have worked as a director and screenwriter. Instead, I went to law school, because "writing does not pay the bills", my dad used to say.

Life made me go back to writing ten years later.

I moved to New York City and discovered a world filled with excitement, dread, endless wonder and relentless change. The Big Apple serves as inspiration for all my stories. I write about my life, hopes, fears, friends and enemies, and anything else that comes to mind.

J.K. Pitcairn

Connect:
Twitter: https://twitter.com/themanicheans
Facebook: https://www.facebook.com/jkpauthor
Blog: http://themanicheans.com/

More to read:
32 Seconds, a YA/Fantasy tale that will be released November 7, 2014. Here's a blurb:

At seventeen years old, Julie Jones is one tormented teenager for whom the glam and glitz of Los Angeles don't mean much anymore. Born troublemaker, she seeks to forget the demons of her past by leaving her family and friends behind. Her journey to a fresh start takes her to the outskirts of a small town where an old lady lures her outside a one-dollar store, and gives her an enchanted chocolate.

After eating the magic piece of candy, Julie enters a parallel universe called the Underworld, where she meets her handsome guide, Evan. Despite her constant struggle to grasp the gravity of her past deeds, and the main reason behind her ill-being, Julie moves on through obstacles and challenges as Evan feeds her answers to many of her questions.

Why does Julie feel like she doesn't belong anywhere? Why does her anger control every one of her actions? Why does she have visions about her best friend Kara, whom she hasn't been in touch with for the past two years? Deep down, Julie knows she won't find peace of mind until she accepts the truth about her anger. And why Kara keeps coming back.

WIPs:

I'm compiling episodes about my alter ego Kiki Reynolds in a novel I hope to release soon, called **Kiki.**

Freshly turned thirty years old, and living in New York City, Kiki likes to tell her life adventures one day at a time. Nothing fancy, nothing crazy, just the reminiscences of a girl whose spirit remains untamed, no matter what other people do to change that. Kiki's proud to be a loner. Well, except when it's Friday night and she's downing scotch only to wake up six hours later with the worst hangover. Kiki should stay away from scotch. And mean girls. And guys who think like stray dogs. So much work to do… Kiki's slowly learning how to be a lady in this world of sharks.

Last but not least, I've been working on a sci-fi/urban fantasy trilogy called **The Manicheans**. First volume to be released in 2015.

By definition, manicheaism is a dualistic philosophy.

The Manicheans are human beings who each possess a supernatural ability. Despite their powers, they live challenging existences, and juggle between good and evil, love and hatred, light and darkness, life and death…

The Manicheans are influenced by another group of supernatural beings called Spirits. The Spirits are subject to the same temptations and choices as the Manicheans. The only difference is that the Spirits can embody any physical appearance they choose, because they're only made of floating atoms.

As one evil Spirit takes over the bodies of several humans to destroy the world by any means possible, the Manicheans and the remaining Spirits must unite to save anything they can, and mostly, themselves.

Along the way, they will face many obstacles, and the battle will take turns no Manichean or Spirit would have thought possible...

www.ingramcontent.com/pod-product-compliance
Lightning Source LLC
Chambersburg PA
CBHW071208130626
46555CB00004B/1631